Little Black Boy

*Oh, the Things
You Will Do!*

To Granny, Grandma Jean and Hoppy. The sum of all parts.
And to our nephews, the world is yours.
—K.H.B. & L.C.F.

Nancy Paulsen Books

An imprint of Penguin Random House LLC, New York

First published in the United States of America by Nancy Paulsen Books,
an imprint of Penguin Random House LLC, 2022

Visit us online at penguinrandomhouse.com

Library of Congress Cataloging-in-Publication Data
Names: Howell-Baptiste, Kirby, author. | Fields, Larry C., III, author. | Davey, Paul, illustrator.
Title: Little Black boy / Kirby Howell-Baptiste and Larry C. Fields III; illustrated by Paul Davey.
Description: New York: Nancy Paulsen Books, 2022. | Summary: "A little Black boy is determined to become a marine biologist and to protect the beaches and oceans sea creatures call home"—Provided by publisher.
Identifiers: LCCN 2022011398 (print) | LCCN 2022011399 (ebook) | ISBN 9780593406267 (hardcover) | ISBN 9780593406281 (kindle edition) | ISBN 9780593406274 (epub)
Subjects: CYAC: Stories in rhyme. | Self-confidence–Fiction. | African Americans–Fiction. | LCGFT: Picture books. | Stories in rhyme.
Classification: LCC PZ8.3.H8379 Lh 2022 (print) | LCC PZ8.3.H8379 (ebook) | DDC [E]–dc23
LC record available at https://lccn.loc.gov/2022011398
LC ebook record available at https://lccn.loc.gov/2022011399

Printed in the United States of America

ISBN 9780593406267
1 3 5 7 9 10 8 6 4 2
PC

Edited by Stacey Barney | Art direction by Cecilia Yung
Design by Eileen Savage | Text set in Intro
The art was done digitally in Clip Studio Paint and Procreate.

Little Black Boy

Oh, the Things You Will Do!

KIRBY HOWELL-BAPTISTE
and LARRY C. FIELDS III

illustrated by PAUL DAVEY

 Nancy Paulsen Books

Little Black Boy, oh, the things you will do.

Has anyone mentioned the world's open to you?

From day one, you began to create
a story you'll live in, no telling how great.

You're here with a purpose; we're so glad you came.

What starts as a spark will turn into a flame.

Your mind is a wonderland, there to explore

endless possibilities; let your imagination soar!

It's okay if you laugh; it's okay if you cry.

It's okay if you miss; what counts is you try.

But as you grow older, fear starts to call,
a little voice inside that says, "You will fall."

But fall you will not, because you are a king.

You know your own heart and that is the thing.

The thing that will guide you and take you so far,

knowing your destiny is to keep raising the bar.

"Toughen up," you may hear, or "Act like a man,"

things you'll be told that you won't understand.

But there's no rush to grow up,

despite what you think.

So savor your youth;

it lasts but a blink.

And speak your mind freely, state what you know.

Watch as they listen and witness your glow.

Whether president or scientist or actor or coach,

you will be an inspiration to all who approach.

Others will see you and they will believe
that anything is possible and they too can achieve.

Knowledge is power, oh, didn't you know?

That's why it's withheld: to ensure you don't grow.

But educate yourself, and know there were others,

a lineage of strength, your fathers and brothers

Men who came before, to help pave the way,
that you may be here and be able to say:

Samuel M. Nabrit

Robert K. Trench

Ernest Everett Just

"I love who I am and I love you all too."

Little Black Boy, oh, the things you will do!